MEET THE PONIES OF PONYVILLE

ORCHARD BOOKS

First published in the US in 2013 by Little, Brown and Company
This edition first published in the UK in 2018 by The Watts Publishing Group

1 3 5 7 9 10 8 6 4 2

A CIP catalogue record for this book is available from the British Library.

ISBN 978 1 40835 240 3

Printed and bound in China

Orchard Books
An imprint of Hachette Children's Group
Part of The Watts Publishing Group Limited
Carmelite House
50 Victoria Embankment
London EC4Y 0DZ

An Hachette UK Company
www.hachette.co.uk

www.hachettechildrens.co.uk

MEET THE PONIES OF PONYVILLE

by Olivia London

ORCHARD

Meet Rainbow Dash!

Look for these words when you read this book. Can you spot them all?

unicorn

letter

orchard

dragon

In the centre of Equestria
is the busy town of Ponyville.
Ponyville is a place
where all kinds of ponies
live together in peace.

Everyone who comes to visit
Equestria makes lots of new friends!
Let's meet the ponies of Ponyville
and learn why everyone loves them!

Twilight Sparkle is an Alicorn. She has strong magical powers, stronger than most Unicorns.

Twilight loves to learn new things.
Princess Celestia is her teacher.
She sent Twilight to Ponyville
to study friendship.

Each week, Twilight has homework.
She writes letters to the princess
about her lessons on friendship.
Twilight always makes sure
her homework is in on time!

Twilight has already learned
that everyone needs friends.
Now she has five best friends!

Spike is a baby dragon.
He lives in the library
with Twilight Sparkle.

He helps Twilight with everything!
Spike even helps her
find books to read for fun!

Spike also helps Twilight
with her homework.
He has a magical way of sending
Twilight's letters to the princess.

Spike loves eating stones that sparkle!
Oh, and he has a secret crush on Rarity.
Shhh!

Rarity is a unicorn.

She is a fashion designer.

She makes a dress for Twilight Sparkle.

Rarity uses her power to find
rare stones for the dress.
She says, "I do not like it –
I love it!"

Rarity owns the Carousel Boutique.

That is where she sells her clothes.

She collects pretty things.

She has a cat called Opal.

Rarity likes to give gifts.

She made everyone the perfect dress

for the Grand Galloping Gala.

Applejack's dress looks fancy!

Applejack loves apples!
She works in the orchard at
Sweet Apple Acres.
Her dog, Winona, helps on the farm!

Applejack makes a lot of
yummy food at the farm.
Applejack often sells the food
at the Ponyville market.

Applejack works hard.

She always tells the truth.

Applejack cheers at the rodeo!

She likes to yell, "Yee-haw!"

Applejack loves playing games,
but she prefers to win –
just like Rainbow Dash!

Rainbow Dash flies
faster than anyone else!
She hopes to be on the
Wonderbolts flying team!

Rainbow Dash can fly so fast that she can change the weather.

Rainbow Dash is a good friend.
But she also likes playing tricks
on other ponies!

She was born in Cloudsdale,
just like Fluttershy.

Fluttershy is graceful and kind.
She loves all animals.
Fluttershy lives near the forest
with her bunny, Angel.

Fluttershy has a special skill
called the Stare.

It calms down wild animals –
even dragons!

She is shy around other ponies.
It is hard to hear Fluttershy
when she speaks.
She is not like Pinkie Pie!

Pinkie Pie has a lot of energy!
She loves to giggle and sing.
She bakes treats for the
Sugarcube Corner bakery.

Pinkie Pie makes ponies smile.

She always says,

"You know what this calls for?

A party!"

Now you know what makes
the Ponyville ponies special.
Come back and visit them soon!